COURTNEY CRUMRIN AND THE PRINCE OF NOWHERE

By
Ted Naifeh

Design by
Ted Naifeh & Keith Wood

Edited by
Joe Nozemack & Jill Beaton

Published by Oni Press, Inc.
Joe Nozemack, publisher
James Lucas Jones, editor in chief
Randal C. Jarrell, managing editor
Cory Casoni, marketing director
Keith Wood, art director
Jill Beaton, assistant editor
Douglas E. Sherwood, production assistant

ONI PRESS, INC.
1305 SE Martin Luther King Jr. Blvd.
Suite A
Portland, OR 97214
USA

www.onipress.com
✦✧✦
www.tednaifeh.com

First edition: December 2008
ISBN 978-1-932664-86-7

1 3 5 7 9 10 8 6 4 2
PRINTED IN CANADA.

THIS FEELING HAD BEEN
COURTNEY'S CONSTANT
COMPANION FOR AS LONG
AS SHE COULD REMEMBER.

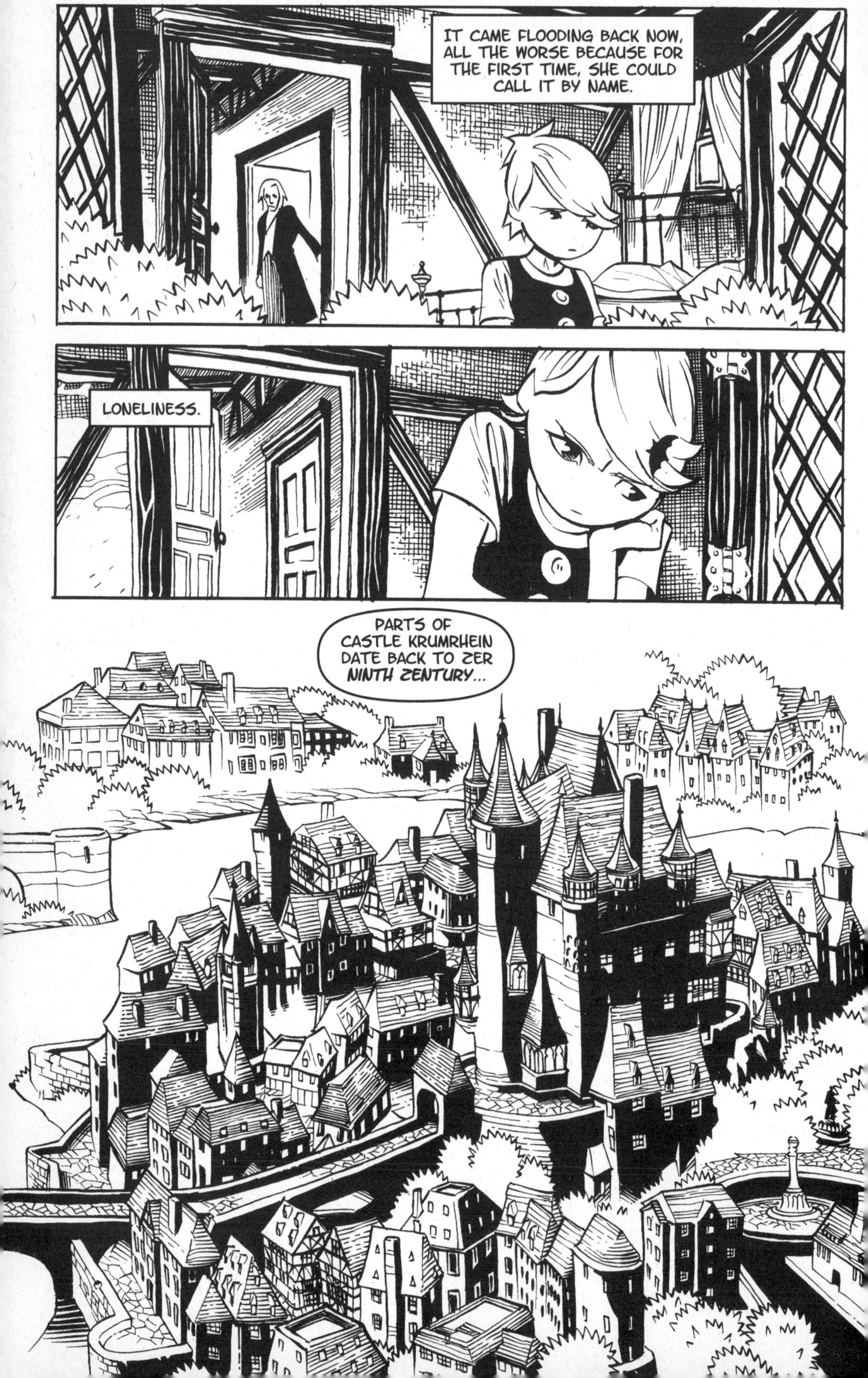
IT CAME FLOODING BACK NOW, ALL THE WORSE BECAUSE FOR THE FIRST TIME, SHE COULD CALL IT BY NAME.
LONELINESS.
PARTS OF CASTLE KRUMRHEIN DATE BACK TO ZER NINTH ZENTURY...

IT VAS VONCE ZER RULING SEAT OFF ZE *HERZOGEN*, THE DUCAL FAMILY UFF KRUMRHEIN VALLEY.

HERE VE HEFF HER GRACE, ZER DUCHESS *ISOLDE VON KRUMRHEIN*...

WHO RULED IN ZE 15TH UNT 16TH ZENTURIES, UNT ISS PERHEPS ZE MOST *VAMOUS* OFF ZER *HERZOGEN*.

OR SHOULT I ZAY ZE MOST *INVAMOUS*?

ZIS VAS PAINTED JUST AFTER ZER *DEATH* UFF HER HUSBANT, HERZOG *LEOPOLT VON KRUMRHEIN*.

LADY *ISOLDE*, ZEN AT ZE AGE OFF *TVENTY*, BECOME OBZESSED MIT ZER *IMMORTALITY*...

...ZURROUNDING HERSELF MIT ZE *ALCHEMISTS* UNT *DARK ZORCERERS* IN A DESPERATE QVEST FOR ZER ZECRET UFF *EVERLASTINK LIFE*.

3

SHE IS KNOWN TO HEFF REIGNED FOR OVER ZEVENTY YEARSS.

TOWARD ZE ENT UFF HER REIGN, A COURTIER WROTE ZET SHE APPEARED *NO DIFFERENT* FROM ZIS PORTRAIT.

ZEY SAY SHE KIDNEPPED *CHILDRENS* FROM ZE TOWN TO DRINK THEIR *BLUT.*

PEASANT SUPERSTITION, NO DOUBT...

...OR *VAS* IT!?!

ZIS VAY PLEASE.

I TAKE IT *YOU'RE* NOT IMPRESSED.

HMM?

LEGEND HESS IT ZET LADY ISOLDE *CONTINUED* TO RULE OVER HER DESCENDANTS FROM BEYOND ZE *GRAVE.*

THE *STORY.* YOU DON'T BUY IT?

DO *YOU?*

DUNNO. I'VE HEARD WEIRDER.

HEARD? OR *SEEN?*

I'M WOLFGANG.

WOLF-?

SORRY?

NOTHING.

...AND I *MYZELF* HAVE ZEEN A TALL, QUEENLY VOOMAN IN BLECK, STANDING JUST BEYOND ZET *DOORVAY.*

AND VONCE *AGAIN* IN ZER VINDOW UFF ZER *NORTH TOWER,* VICH HESS BEEN INACCESSIBLE FOR *ZENTURIES,* EXZEPT BY HELICOPTER.

THAT ONE GOES AROUND *CORNERS,* RIGHT?

THE *KNIGHT,* YES. YOU'VE *TRULY* NEVER BEFORE PLAYED *CHESS?*

5

MY PARENTS PREFER GAMES WITH BRIGHTLY COLORED MONEY.

CHECKMATE.

OH, OKAY. I SHOULD MOVE MY KING AGAIN, RIGHT?

NO. THE GAME IS FINISHED.

BUT... BUT YOU HAVEN'T TAKEN MY KING. I THOUGHT THAT WAS THE POINT.

I DON'T HAVE TO. HE HAS NOWHERE TO GO, YOU SEE?

HUH...

I'M GLAD YOU'RE ENJOYING THE CASTLE...

BUT I'D RATHER YOU DIDN'T SHOW YOUR APPRECIATION BY GETTING EJECTED.

WHAT ARE YOU DOING?

>KNOCK<
>KNOCK<
>KNOCK<

YEAH?

I JUST WANTED...

I...

I WAS JUST GOING TO RETIRE. IS THERE ANYTHING YOU NEED?

I'M FINE.

VERY WELL.

IT WASN'T THAT SHE HATED HER UNCLE. SHE FELT SORRY FOR HIM.

AFTER A LIFETIME OF ISOLATION, THE MAN HAD THE EMOTIONAL EMPATHY OF A WEEVIL.

SHE JUST COULDN'T TRUST HIM ANYMORE. SHE COULDN'T TRUST ANYONE.

WHICH WAS PROBABLY HOW ALOYSIUS HAD ENDED UP THE WAY HE WAS.

OH, HELLO.

WHO'S THERE?

ONLY ME. ARE YOU ALL RIGHT?

YOU LOOK, I DON'T KNOW, WORRIED PERHAPS?

EXISTENTIAL ANGST.

WHAT IS THIS?

HECK IF I KNOW. YOU'RE THE ONE WHO SPEAKS GERMAN.

HAVE YOU EVER *LOVED* ANYONE?

A *GIRL*, YOU MEAN?

ANYONE. DO YOU LOVE YOUR *PARENTS*?

DOESN'T *EVERYONE*?

WHAT DOES IT EVEN *MEAN*, THOUGH? I DON'T THINK *I* FEEL ONE WAY OR THE *OTHER* ABOUT MY FOLKS. NOT *REALLY*.

THEY'RE JUST THESE... PEOPLE.

I KEEP HEARING ABOUT SOMETHING CALLED *"UNCONDITIONAL LOVE."* IT'S SUPPOSED TO FEEL LIKE THIS BIG WARM *HUG* ALL DAY LONG OR SOMETHING.

I NEVER FELT *ANYTHING* LIKE THAT. NOT ABOUT *ANYBODY*. PEOPLE LET YOU *DOWN*. THEY BREAK YOUR *HEART*.

THEY *DIE* ON YOU.

DYING IS NOT THE WORST THING.

I LOVE MY MOTHER. BUT AFTER MY FATHER DIED, SHE SEALED UP HER HEART, LITTLE BY LITTLE.

NOW SHE FEELS NOTHING.

THE HEART MUST FEEL. TO BE STRONG, IT MUST BLEED.

THEY SEAL IT TO STOP THE PAIN. THEN THE BLOOD INSIDE ROTS AND TURNS TO SLUDGE, AND THE HEART SHRIVELS UP LIKE AN OLD APPLE.

THANKS FOR THE IMAGE. WHO DO YOU MEAN?

GROWN-UPS.

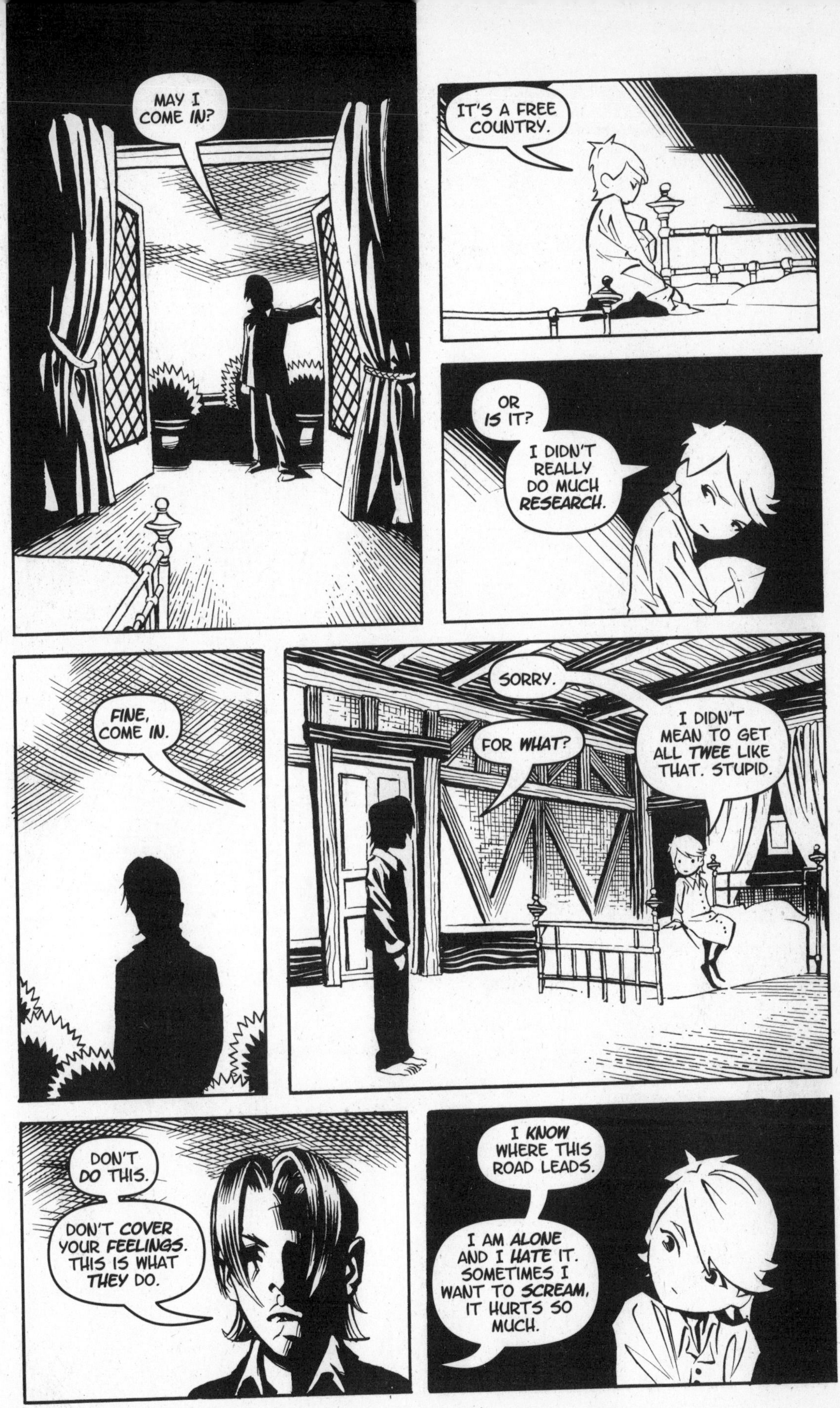
MAY I COME *IN*?
IT'S A FREE COUNTRY.
OR *IS* IT?
I DIDN'T REALLY DO MUCH *RESEARCH*.
FINE, COME *IN*.
SORRY.
FOR *WHAT*?
I DIDN'T MEAN TO GET ALL *TWEE* LIKE THAT. STUPID.
DON'T *DO* THIS.
DON'T *COVER* YOUR *FEELINGS*. THIS IS WHAT *THEY* DO.
I *KNOW* WHERE THIS ROAD LEADS.
I AM *ALONE* AND I *HATE* IT. SOMETIMES I WANT TO *SCREAM*, IT HURTS SO MUCH.

BUT I FEEL NO *SHAME* FOR WHAT I NEED.

WHAT DO YOU NEED?

A FRIEND.

SOMEONE WHO *CARES* FOR ME.

LOOK, I'M *SORRY.* I JUST...

I...

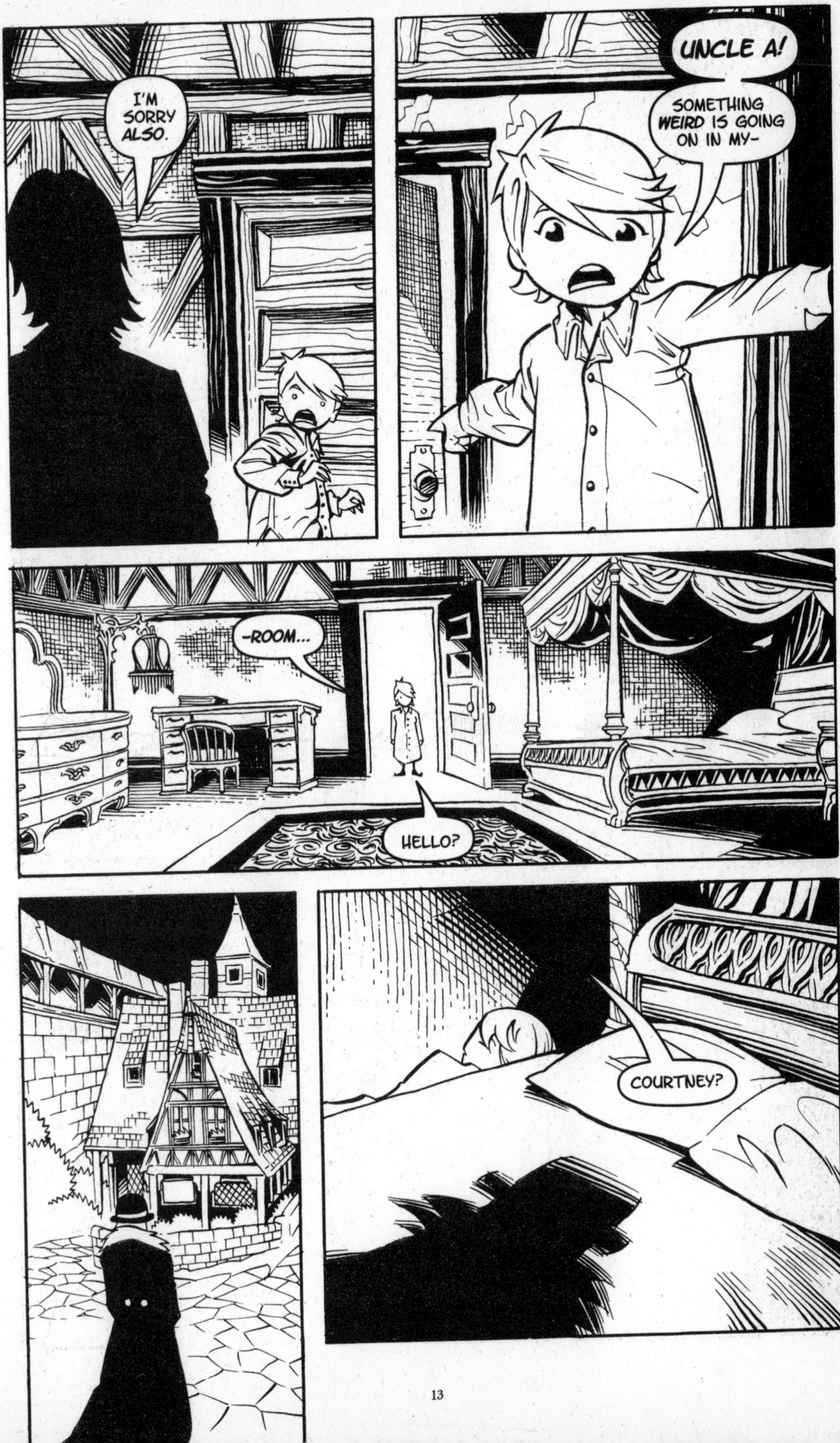
I'M SORRY ALSO.
UNCLE A!
SOMETHING WEIRD IS GOING ON IN MY-
-ROOM...
HELLO?
COURTNEY?

WHAT ARE YOU DOING IN *HERE*?

ARE YOU ALL *RIGHT*?

I— I WAS...

I GOT *SCARED*. WHERE WERE YOU?

SCARED? *YOU*? I FIND THAT HARD TO BELIEVE.

WHAT COULD THE NIGHT HOLD THAT'S MORE FRIGHTENING THAN *COURTNEY CRUMRIN*?

HE HAD A POINT, OF COURSE. YET SOMEHOW, THIS WASN'T THE REACTION COURTNEY WAS HOPING FOR.

YEAH, *RIGHT*. SORRY TO BOTHER YOU.

OKAY, MISTER SMOOTH-TALKER GHOST GUY. I HOPE YOU KNOW WHO YOU'RE *DEALING WITH*.

'CAUSE WHATEVER YOU ARE *NOW*, MESS WITH ME AND I'LL TURN YOU INTO A PURPLE ARMADILLO.

WHAT IS THIS AWMER -DILLO?

I *KNOW* WHAT YOU ARE. I COULD NOT *HURT* YOU, EVEN IF I HAD *WANTED* IT.

SO WHAT'S YOUR STORY? I CAN *TOUCH* YOU, WHICH MEANS YOU'RE NOT A *GHOST*.

WHICH LEAVES...

...VAMPIRE?

ARE YOU ANGRY?

NAW. I GUESS AFTER A FEW HUNDRED YEARS, IT'S NICE TO TALK TO SOMEONE NEW.

IT WAS DISORIENTING. BEING THOUSANDS OF MILES FROM ANYTHING FAMILIAR WAS STRANGE ENOUGH.

BUT COURTNEY DIDN'T EVEN REALLY FEEL SHE HAD A HOME TO RETURN TO ANYMORE.

SHE FELT LIKE A LOST SHIP AFTER ALL THE CONTINENTS HAD SUNK UNDER THE SEA.

ZE FIRE VASS STARTED BY ZE ANGRY MOB OFF TOWN FOLK WHO BELIEVED ZE CATHEDRAL A HAVEN FOR ZE VORSHIPPERS OFF ZATAN...

...UNT BLAMED ZEM FOR ZE VANISHED CHILDREN.

...WONDERING IF THERE WERE ANY OTHER SHIPS OUT THERE ON THE ENDLESS, EMPTY OCEAN.

I THOUGHT DAYTIME WASN'T YOUR *SCENE*.

I AM COMPLICATED.

APPARENTLY.

THIS ONE WAS A TERRIBLE DESPOT. HE *BURNED* HALF THE TOWN TRYING TO ENFORCE HIS MAD *TAX LAWS*.

THIS ONE WAS *KIND*. BEING DUKE WAS ONLY EVER A *BURDEN* TO HIM. HE WAS *MURDERED* BY HIS OWN *ADVISORS* BEFORE HE WAS *TWENTY*.

WHO'S BURIED HERE?

ME.

BUT ONLY SOMETIMES.

THANK YOU FOR *MEETING* ME AGAIN.

WELL, I WAS *THINKING* OF GOING OUT *CLOG DANCING* WITH MY *UNCLE*...

...BUT YOU'RE BETTER COMPANY.

IS *THIS* WHAT HE TOLD YOU? THAT HE IS *DANCING*?

I WAS *JOKING*... WAIT! YOU KNOW WHERE HE GOES AT NIGHT?

HE WENT TO THE *CASTLE*?

HE HAS KNOWN MY *MOTHER* FOR MANY YEARS.

THE DUCHESS? LADY *ISOLDE*?

THEY TALK FOR *HOURS* OF *ALCHEMY* AND OTHER DULL THINGS.

GEE, THANKS FOR INVITING ME...

SHE LIKES TO KEEP TRACK OF THE *FAMILY*, ESPECIALLY THE ONES WITH A LITTLE *MAGIC*.

HOLD ON... *KRUMRHEIN?* YOU MEAN...

HE'S, LIKE, A *DESCENDANT?*

THAT'S RIGHT.

SO I'M ALSO, LIKE, A VON *KRUMRHEIN?*

WOULD YOU LIKE TO SEE THE *CASTLE* AGAIN? THE NORTH *TOWER*, PERHAPS?

YOU GOTTA BE KIDDING...

WOW. *THAT'S* A HANDY TRICK.

19

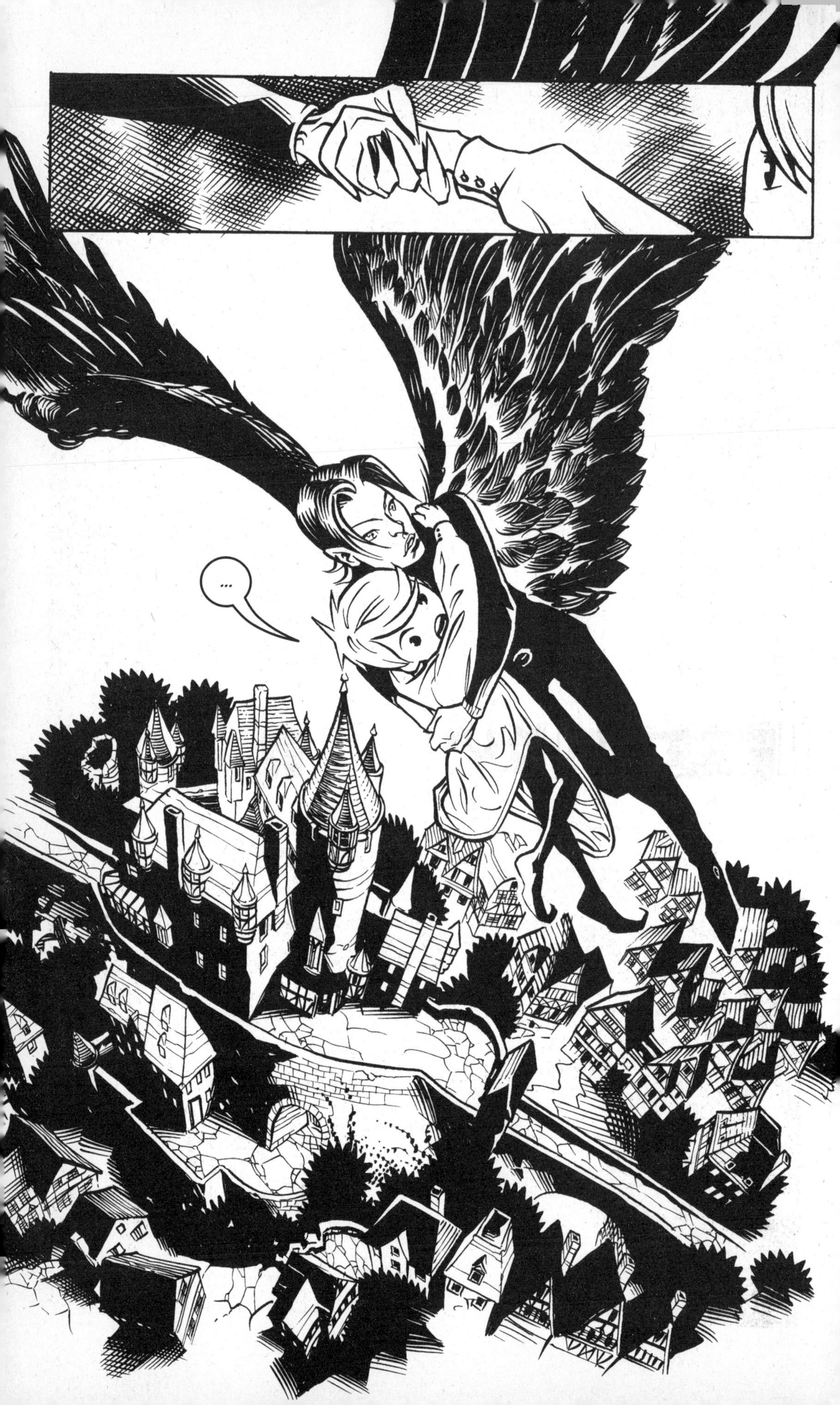
...

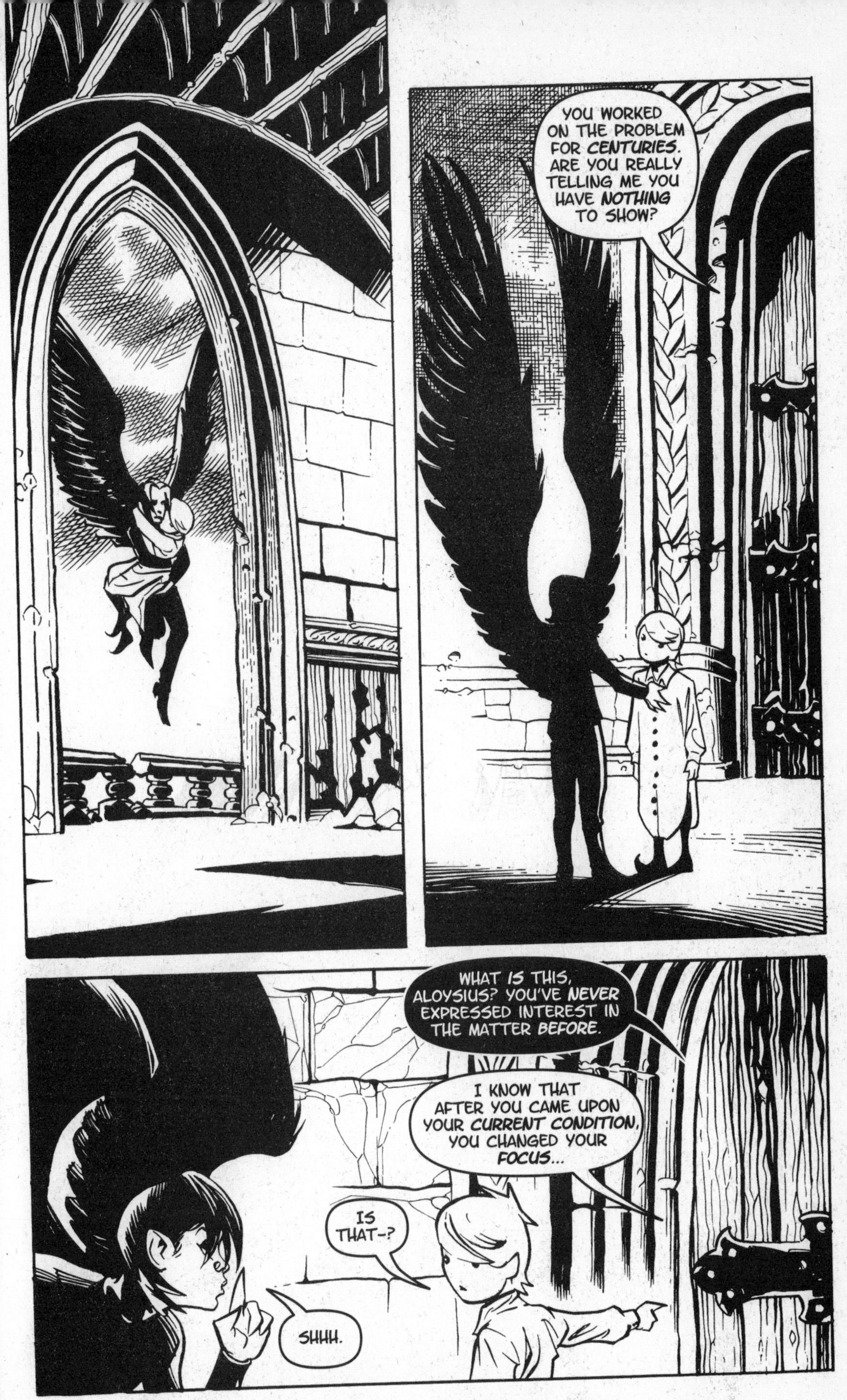

YOU WORKED ON THE PROBLEM FOR CENTURIES. ARE YOU REALLY TELLING ME YOU HAVE NOTHING TO SHOW?
WHAT IS THIS, ALOYSIUS? YOU'VE NEVER EXPRESSED INTEREST IN THE MATTER BEFORE.
I KNOW THAT AFTER YOU CAME UPON YOUR CURRENT CONDITION, YOU CHANGED YOUR FOCUS...
IS THAT-?
SHHH.

TO A DEGREE, YES.

...SEEKING A MEANS OF RESTORING YOUR... HOW TO PHRASE IT...

MY HUMANITY?

I WOULDN'T HAVE PUT IT *THAT* WAY.

TIME WAS *RUNNING OUT*. MY ELIXIRS HAD CEASED TO BE *EFFECTIVE*.

I WAS *GROWING OLD*, ALOYSIUS. *WITHERING*. I NEEDED A *DRASTIC SOLUTION*.

YOU WERE *THIRTY-FIVE*, MADAM. HARDLY WHAT I'D CALL *DIRE STRAITS*.

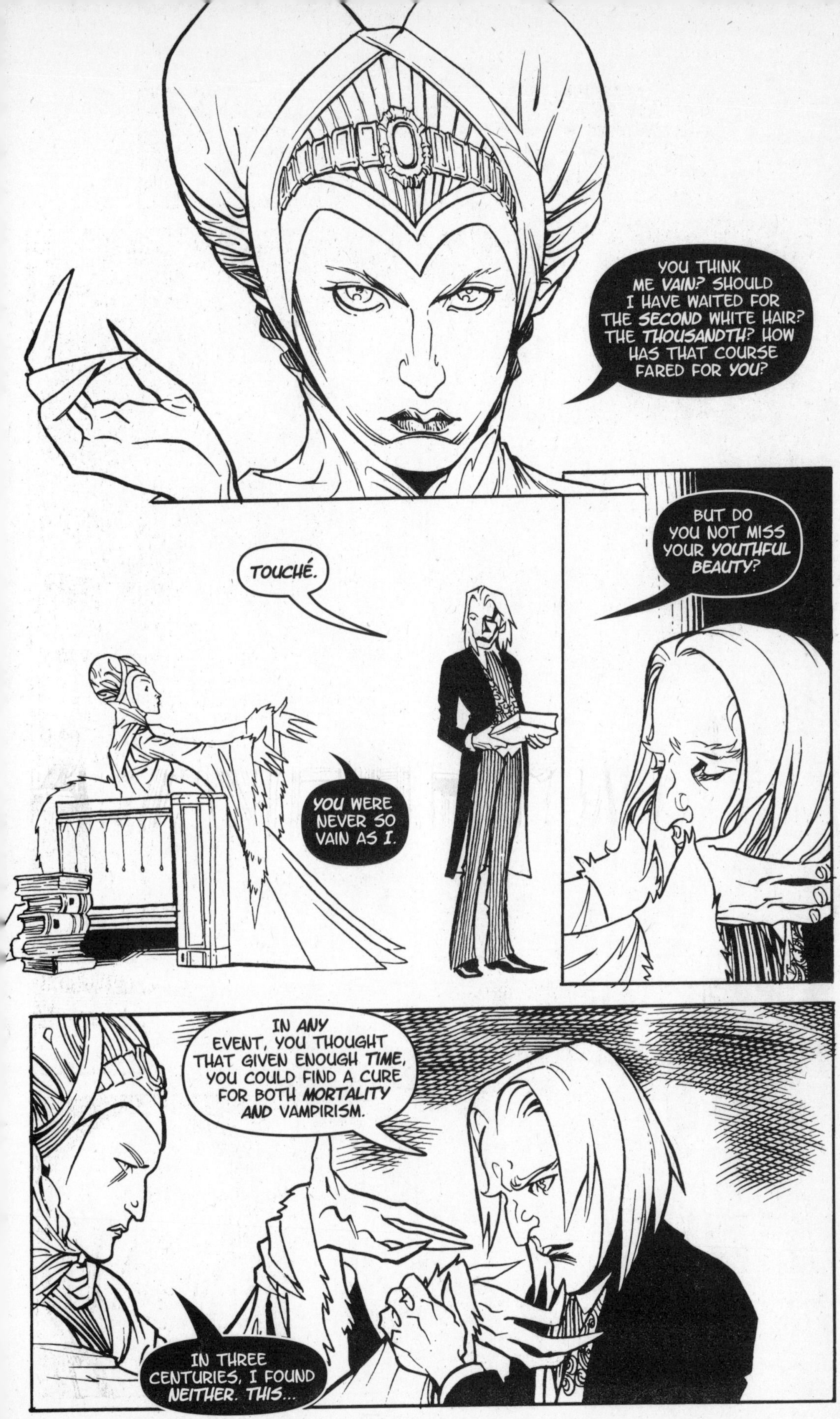
YOU THINK ME VAIN? SHOULD I HAVE WAITED FOR THE SECOND WHITE HAIR? THE THOUSANDTH? HOW HAS THAT COURSE FARED FOR YOU?
TOUCHÉ.
YOU WERE NEVER SO VAIN AS I.
BUT DO YOU NOT MISS YOUR YOUTHFUL BEAUTY?
IN ANY EVENT, YOU THOUGHT THAT GIVEN ENOUGH TIME, YOU COULD FIND A CURE FOR BOTH MORTALITY AND VAMPIRISM.
IN THREE CENTURIES, I FOUND NEITHER. THIS...

...IS THE ONLY CURE FOR MORTALITY.

TAKE IT OR *LEAVE* IT.

I TOLD YOU BEFORE, I'LL HAVE NO PART OF...

...THAT FORM OF IMMORTALITY.

YOU *SNEER*, MY *ARROGANT* CHILD. YET YOU *COME* TO ME *AGAIN* AFTER THREE DECADES...

AS DESPERATE AS *I* ONCE WAS.

WHAT DRIVES YOU *HITHER*, IF NOT *VANITY*?

FOR SOME YEARS NOW, I'VE PURSUED *SEVERAL* LINES OF INQUIRY REGARDING A RATHER *MUNDANE* MALADY.

MY CRAFT CAN ONLY DELAY THE INEVITABLE, AND MY CLINIC IN *SWITZERLAND* HAS EXHAUSTED ITS RESEARCHES.

IT APPEARS THAT, WITHIN A YEAR, MY *HEART* WILL FAIL.

UNLESS I FIND A *MIRACLE.*

OLD FOOL. SO FULL OF *SCORN* ONCE, AND NOW...

DEATH IS HUMANITY'S *JESTER,* ALOYSIUS. HE MAKES FOOLS OF US ALL, LAUGHING AT OUR PRETENDED *MAJESTY.*

THIS IS THE *LAST* OF MY *ELIXIR VITAE*. I DON'T KNOW *WHY* I HELD ONTO IT FOR SO *LONG.*

TAKE IT, CHILD. IN MEMORY OF WHAT WE *MIGHT* HAVE BEEN TO ONE ANOTHER.

DO I WANT TO KNOW WHAT'S IN IT?

NO.

IT WILL ONLY *DELAY* THE INEVITABLE, ALOYSIUS.

IT WILL PULL YOU FROM THE *BRINK.*

BUT THE GROUND *CRUMBLES* BENEATH YOUR FEET, AND SOMEDAY, YOU MUST FALL.

UNLESS, LIKE *ANGELS,* YOU LEARN HOW TO *FLY.*

MY FOLKS USED TO MAKE ME PLAY *MONOPOLY* WITH THEM. THEY WERE REALLY *GOOD* AT IT.

BETTER THAN I WAS, ANYWAY.

I'D START OFF WITH A LITTLE MONEY AND ALL THESE *HOPES*. BUT BEFORE LONG, MY MOM WOULD BUY *BOARDWALK*, AND I JUST KNEW I WAS *DOOMED*.

COURTNEY TRIED TO SORT IT ALL OUT IN HER HEAD, BUT IT WAS USELESS. EVERY KIND OF HOPE AND FEAR SHE'D EVER KNOWN CAME CRASHING THROUGH IN A TANGLED, IMPOSSIBLE MESS.

THING IS, THE GAME WOULD KEEP *GOING* AND *GOING* FOR HOURS.

I'M WATCHING MY MONEY *DWINDLE*, MY DEBTS PILE UP, MY LITTLE *TRIUMPHS* GETTING SOLD OFF...

...AND MY FOLKS SMIRKING.

I LIKE THIS GAME *BETTER*. WHEN YOU KNOW YOU CAN'T *WIN*, IT'S OVER.

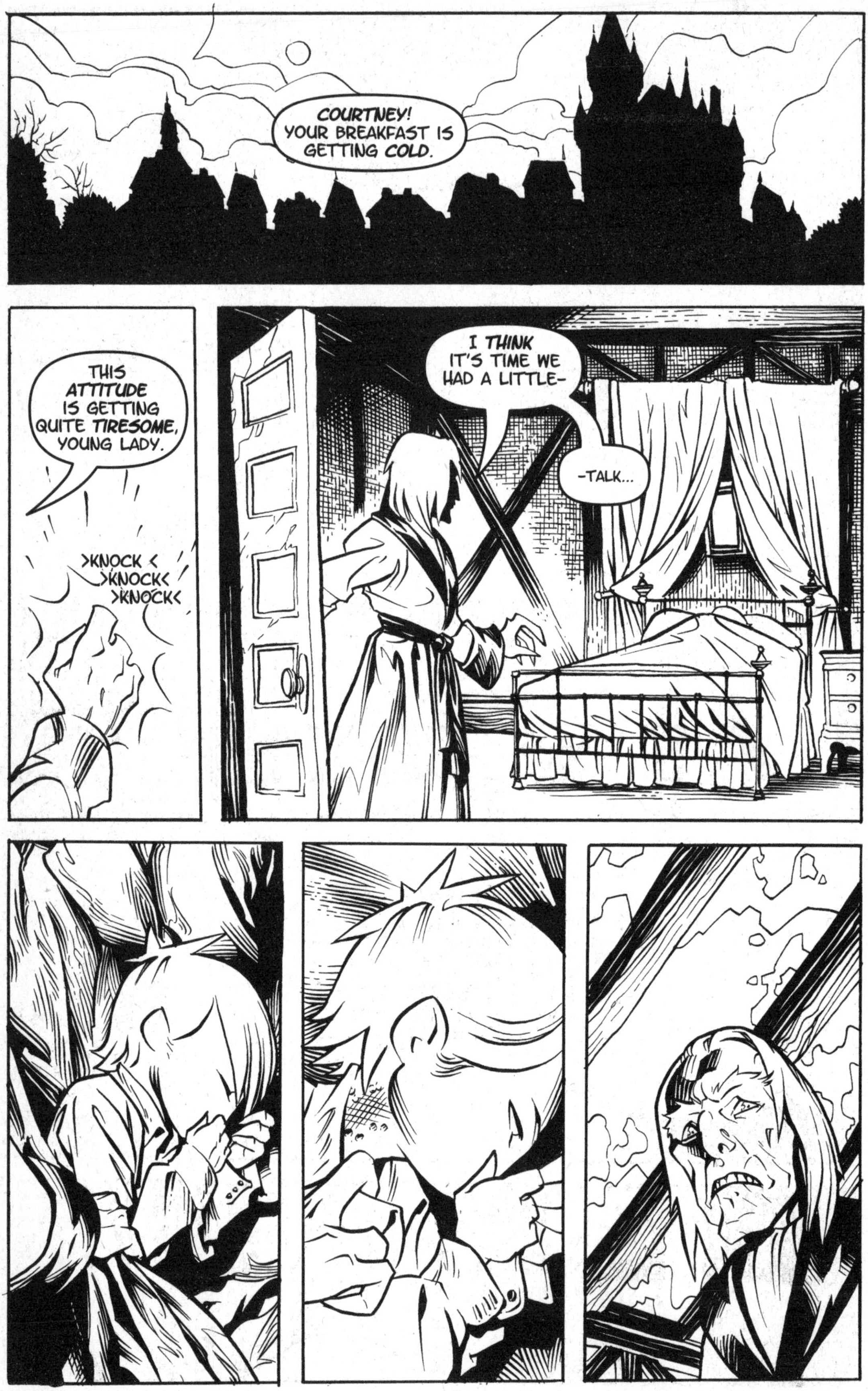
COURTNEY! YOUR BREAKFAST IS GETTING COLD.
THIS ATTITUDE IS GETTING QUITE TIRESOME, YOUNG LADY.
>KNOCK< >KNOCK< >KNOCK<
I THINK IT'S TIME WE HAD A LITTLE-
-TALK...

IT'S A BIT OF AN EMERGENCY, I'M AFRAID.

DON'T VORRY, HERR PROFESSOR.

VE ARE A FULL SERVICE ESTABLISHMENT.

AND I'LL HAVE TO GET TO ZE MARKET BEFORE IT CLOSES. FRESH GARLIC IS MOST EFFECTIVE.

ONE OF US SHOULD WATCH HER AT ALL TIMES.

JUST VOR A CHANGE, DO YOU MEAN?

LOOK *HERE*, MADAM, THIS ISN'T MY *FAULT*. HAD COURTNEY BEEN AN *ORDINARY* GIRL, IT WOULD BE *ONE* THING. BUT SHE'S *CERTAINLY* MORE THAN A MATCH FOR SOME CHEEKY VAMPIRE BRAT.

SHE'S A CHILD, YOU ASS! A CHILD!

SHE'S WULNERABLE IN VAYS ZET HEFF NOTHING TO DO WISS POWER.

AND YOU'VE BEEN *TREATING* HER LIKE A PIECE OF INCONWENIENT *BAGGAGE*.

SHE DOESN'T USUALLY *ACT* LIKE A CHILD. SHE'S SO... MATURE.

ZMALL WONDER.

SHE PROBABLY HAD TO GROW UP *FAST*. AFTER ALL, WHO TAKES *CARE* OFF HER?

I'VE GOT TO GET TO ZE *MARKET*. FOR *HEAVEN'S* SAKE, DON'T GO VANDERING OFF AGAIN TILL I GET BECK.

I DON'T WANT TO BE *RUDE*, BUT DOES ANY OF THIS STUFF *WORK*? AND WHAT'S WITH THE *CRACKERS* UNDER THE *WINDOW*?

SACRED *WAFERS*, LIEBCHEN. *ZER BODY* OFF OUR *LORD*. MY *PRIEST* VAS KIND ENOUGH TO *TRANSUBSTANTIATE* ZEM IN CASE OF AN *EMERGENCY*.

THAT WAS *NICE* OF HIM. BUT DON'T THEY ONLY WORK IF I *BELIEVE* IN THEM OR SOMETHING?

DON'T YOU?

IN *CRACKERS*? NOT REALLY.

ALOYSIUS SAID THAT CHRISTIAN MAGIC CAN *WORK*, BUT ONLY IF YOU BUY INTO THE WHOLE *SON OF GOD* THING, AT LEAST A *LITTLE* BIT. WHICH I *DON'T*.

SORRY. NO OFFENSE.

NONE *TAKEN*. IT DOESN'T METTER VAT *YOU* BELIEF. IT'S VAT YOUR LITTLE *FRIEND* BELIEVES ZET COUNTS.

YOU MEAN *WOLFGANG*? NOW YOU *REALLY* LOST ME.

YOUR *UNCLE HESS* TAUGHT YOU ZE *OLD* MAGIC, FROM BEFORE ZE WORD OFF ZE *LORD* CAME TO EUROPE.

BUT ZE *LORD'S* POWER ISN'T SO DIFFERENT. IT HESS ITS DARK SIDE *TOO*, LIKE *YOURS*.

IT *DOES*?

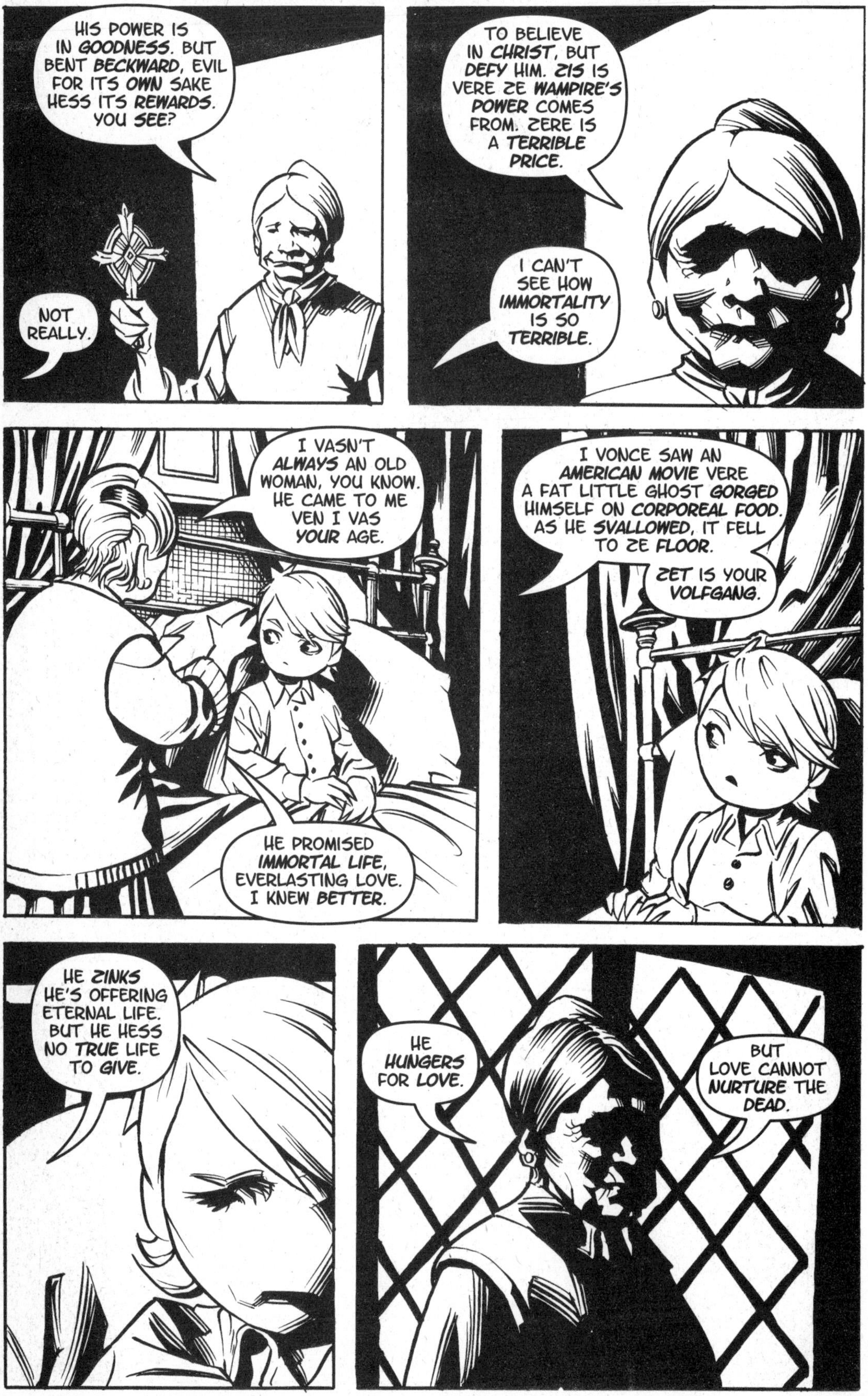
HIS POWER IS IN GOODNESS. BUT BENT BECKWARD, EVIL FOR ITS OWN SAKE HESS ITS REWARDS. YOU SEE?
NOT REALLY.
TO BELIEVE IN CHRIST, BUT DEFY HIM. ZIS IS VERE ZE WAMPIRE'S POWER COMES FROM. ZERE IS A TERRIBLE PRICE.
I CAN'T SEE HOW IMMORTALITY IS SO TERRIBLE.
I VASN'T ALWAYS AN OLD WOMAN, YOU KNOW. HE CAME TO ME VEN I VAS YOUR AGE.
HE PROMISED IMMORTAL LIFE, EVERLASTING LOVE. I KNEW BETTER.
I VONCE SAW AN AMERICAN MOVIE VERE A FAT LITTLE GHOST GORGED HIMSELF ON CORPOREAL FOOD. AS HE SVALLOWED, IT FELL TO ZE FLOOR.
ZET IS YOUR VOLFGANG.
HE ZINKS HE'S OFFERING ETERNAL LIFE. BUT HE HESS NO TRUE LIFE TO GIVE.
HE HUNGERS FOR LOVE.
BUT LOVE CANNOT NURTURE THE DEAD.

COURTNEY WASN'T SURE IF SHE WAS SEEING THINGS IN THIS WORLD ANYMORE.

WAS SHE STARING INTO HELL?

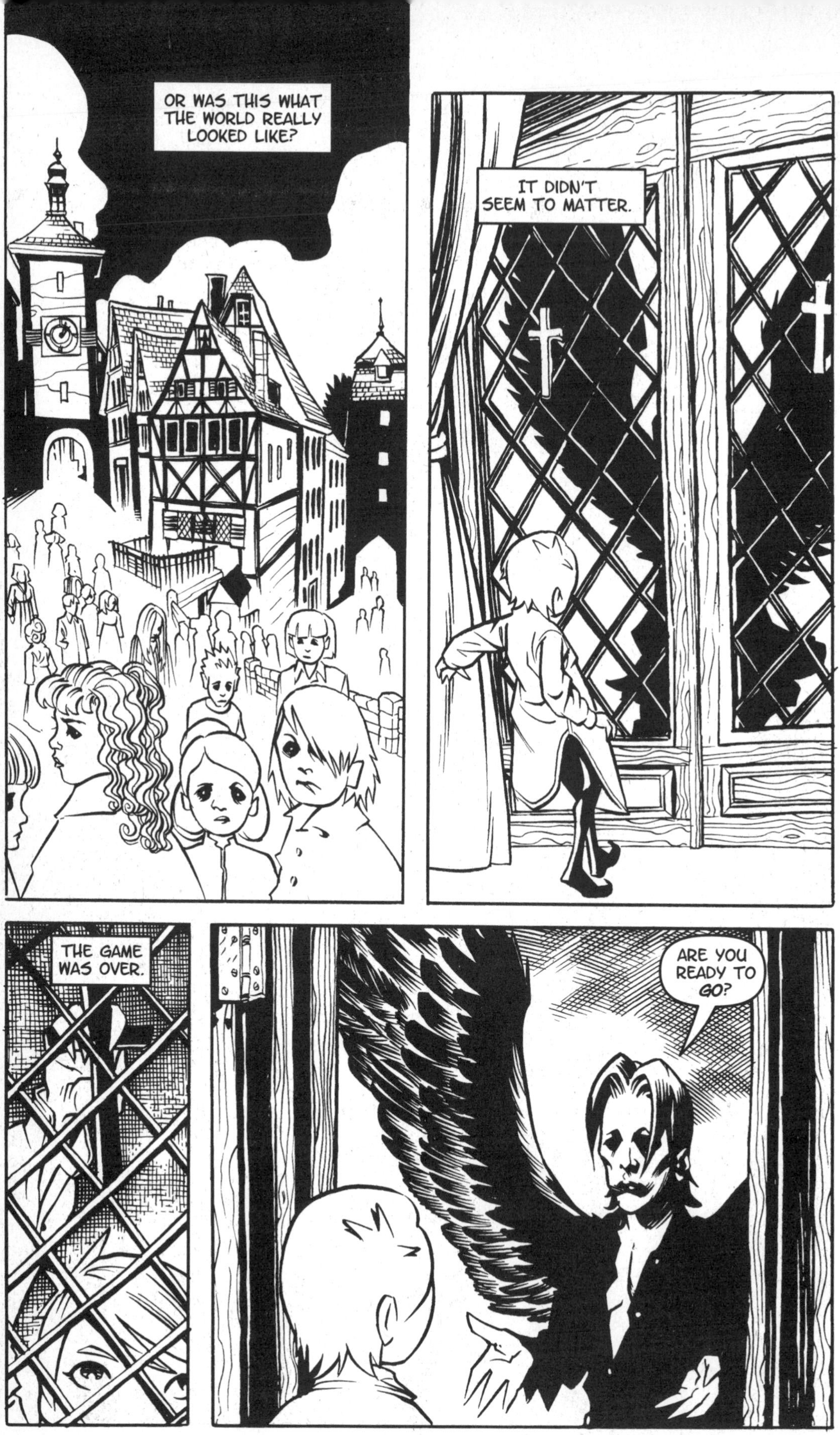
OR WAS THIS WHAT THE WORLD REALLY LOOKED LIKE?
IT DIDN'T SEEM TO MATTER.
THE GAME WAS OVER.
ARE YOU READY TO GO?

FORGETTING SOMETHING?

YOU'RE SUPPOSED TO *SUCK UP* TO HER OLD MAN.

RAAAAAAA

Thunk

ARRRRGHH

GAAH!

GET DOWN!

GRRROOOWWLLL

STALE *TRICKS*, BOY. HAVEN'T YOU LEARNED ANYTHING *NEW* OVER THE CENTURIES?

RAAAAAACCCHHHH

UNCLE A?

AND *THIS* TRICK? TOO *OLD* FOR YOU?

DON'T *HURT* HIM!

CAN YOU FLY, MORTAL?

OF *COURSE* I CAN FLY, YOU NINCOMPOOP. I'M A *WARLOCK.*

...

BOOOMMM

YOUR CONCERN *WAS* TOUCHING, I *MUST* SAY. THOUGH I FEAR YOUR *PLEAS* FELL ON *DEAF EARS.*

NO KIDDING. I WASN'T TALKING TO HIM.

IT ISN'T OVER. HE VON'T STOP NOW.

WE CAN BE GONE BY NIGHTFALL TOMORROW.

SHE'S IN NO SHAPE TO TRAVEL. BESIDES, IT VON'T METTER. HER BLOOD CALLS TO HIM.

HE'LL FOLLOW HER ACROSS ZE VORLD. UNLESS HE'S DESTROYED.

OR SHE FORSAKES HIM UTTERLY.

COURTNEY, YOU SAW WHAT HE IS. YOU DON'T WANT ANYTHING TO DO WITH HIM, DO YOU?

JUST CLOSE YOUR HEART TO HIM, AND IT'LL BE OVER.

GO TO HELL.

I REPLACED THE *CROSSES* AND NAILED UP THE *DOORS*. THEY *SHOULD* HOLD.

NOT IF SHE WANTS *OUT*.

I'M GOING FOR A *WALK*. KEEP AN EYE ON HER TILL I GET *BACK*.

YOU SHOULD BE IN *BED*.

I'M NOT *HUNGRY*.

YOU VILL BE *LATER*, VONE VAY OR ZE OTHER.

YOU SAW ZE *CHILDREN*, DIDN'T YOU?

YES.

THEN YOU KNOW WHAT YOU MUST *BECOME*.

SURELY YOUR LIFE ISN'T SO BAD THAT ETERNAL *HOPELESSNESS* SEEMS BETTER.

I'M *SICK* OF HOPE. I KNOW WHERE IT *LEADS*.

YEAR AFTER YEAR, HOPING THAT SOMEONE WILL COME ALONG WHO DOESN'T LET ME *DOWN*.

UNTIL I'M *GOD KNOWS* HOW OLD AND TRYING TO HOLD OFF *DEATH* JUST A LITTLE LONGER. FOR *WHAT*?

LOSING SHOULDN'T TAKE THAT *LONG*.

WHAT ARE *YOU* DOING HERE?

I SHOULD THINK IT *OBVIOUS*.

>SNORT<

VERDAMMT!

YOU THINK YOU CAN DEFEAT ME, MORTAL?

I CAN BECOME *WOLF*, *BIRD OF PREY*, *VAPOR*. YOUR FIRE, YOUR *SWORD*, YOUR *WOODEN STAKES*...

THESE THINGS CANNOT HARM VAPOR.

I DON'T INTEND TO *FIGHT* YOU.

I'M JUST WAITING TO SEE WHICH GRAVE YOU RETURN TO.

OTHERWISE I'D BE ALL DAY SEARCHING.

I'M FAMILIAR WITH YOUR POWERS. ALL OF THEM.

MOST ARE JUST SORCERER'S TRICKS YOUR MOTHER TAUGHT YOU.

TOO BAD YOU'RE SUCH A POOR STUDENT.

STOP IT!

LEAVE HIM ALONE, PLEASE! CAN'T YOU SEE HE'S ALREADY HURT!?!

COURTNEY! YOU SHOULDN'T BE HERE!

SO YOU CAN PLAY YOUR LITTLE GAMES IN SECRET? LIKE IN ROMANIA?

I ONLY MEANT TO KEEP YOU OUT OF DANGER. I DIDN'T WANT YOU TO SEE THIS.

SEE WHAT? THAT YOU'RE A BULLY?

LOOK, YOU'VE WON. YOU DON'T HAVE TO MAKE IT WORSE.

I'M USED TO THIS CRAP FROM MY PARENTS.

BUT ALL THESE STUPID GAMES...

YOU WERE SUPPOSED TO KNOW BETTER.

YOU'RE RIGHT. I'M SORRY.

I'VE NEVER BEEN GOOD AT TAKING CARE OF ANYONE.

OBVIOUSLY.

I DON'T NEED TAKEN CARE OF. I JUST...

I DON'T KNOW.

I QUITE UNDERSTAND.

45

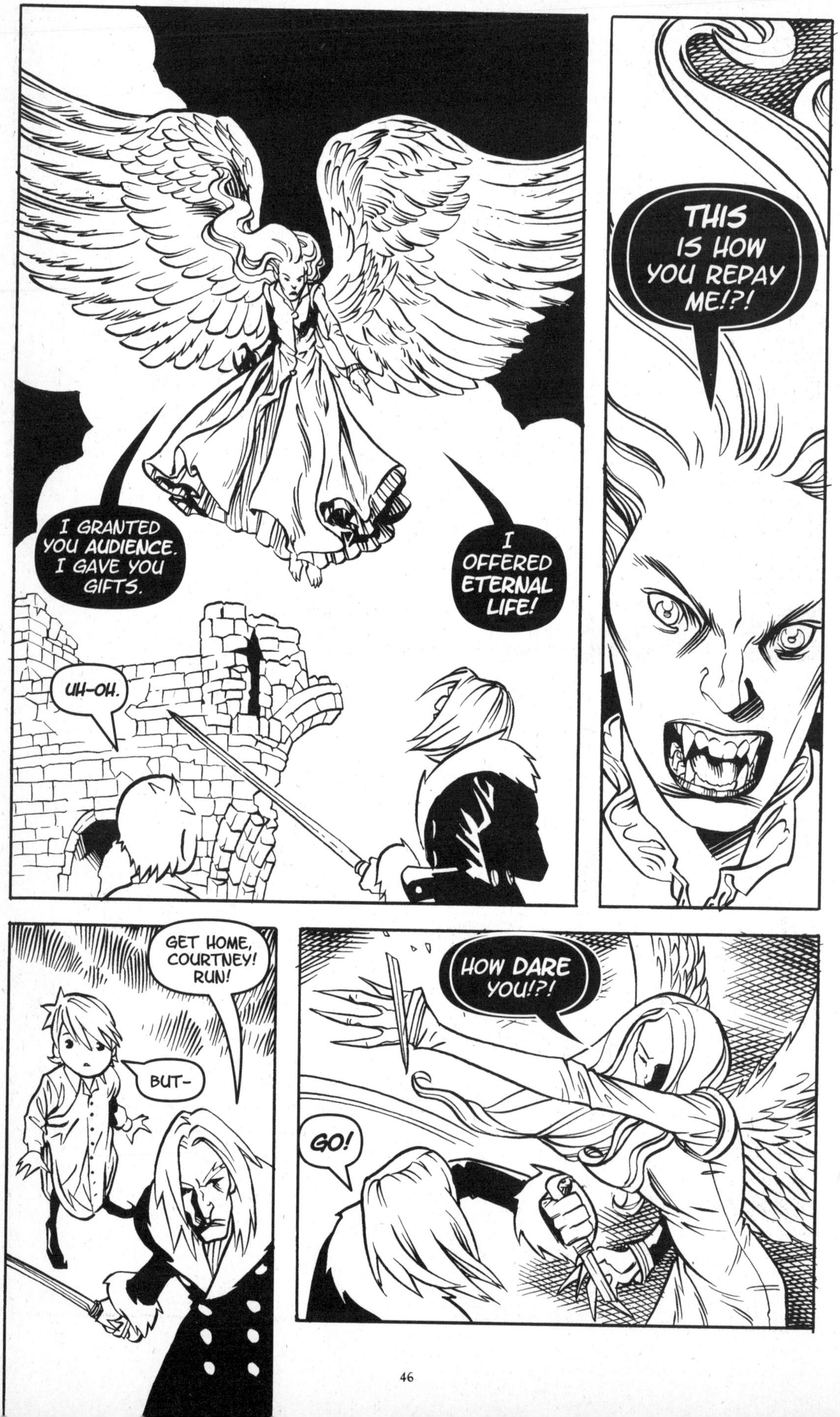
I GRANTED YOU AUDIENCE. I GAVE YOU GIFTS.
I OFFERED ETERNAL LIFE!
UH-OH.
THIS IS HOW YOU REPAY ME!?!
GET HOME, COURTNEY! RUN!
BUT-
HOW DARE YOU!?!
GO!

MY POWERS MAY BE ONLY SORCERY AS YOU SAY...

BUT I'VE HAD CENTURIES TO HONE THEM.

VERY WELL.

LET US SEE WHO'S THE BETTER SORCERER.

YOU TRICKY...

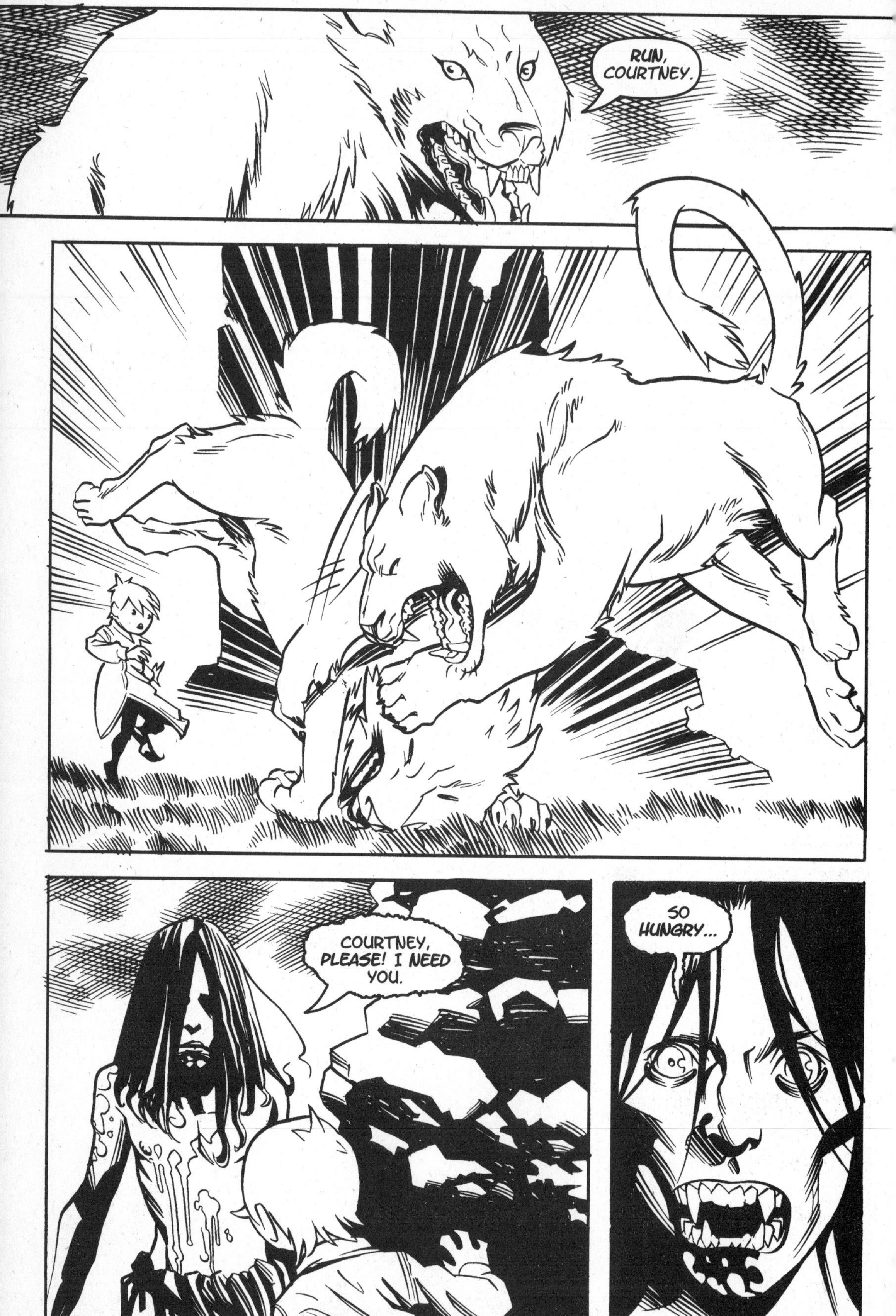
RUN, COURTNEY.
COURTNEY, PLEASE! I NEED YOU.
SO HUNGRY...

IS THIS WHAT YOU WANTED, ALOYSIUS?

IS THIS BETTER THAN LIFE EVERLASTING?

MAYBE NOT.

BUT THE VIEW IS BETTER.

VOOOMMM

WE'LL BE TOGETHER FOREVER.

WE'LL NEVER BE LONELY AGAIN.

I BET YOU SAY THAT TO ALL THE GIRLS.

SORRY, UNCLE A. IT'S TOO LATE.

THREE BITES.

GAME OVER.

CHECKMATE.

IT'S NOT LIKE YOU TO GIVE UP SO EASILY.

THE TRICK IS TO CHANGE THE RULES.

WHAT GAME YOU'RE PLAYING IS UP TO YOU.

HERE.

YOU MIGHT FIND THIS USEFUL.

©1936

Chance
GET OUT OF JAIL FREE

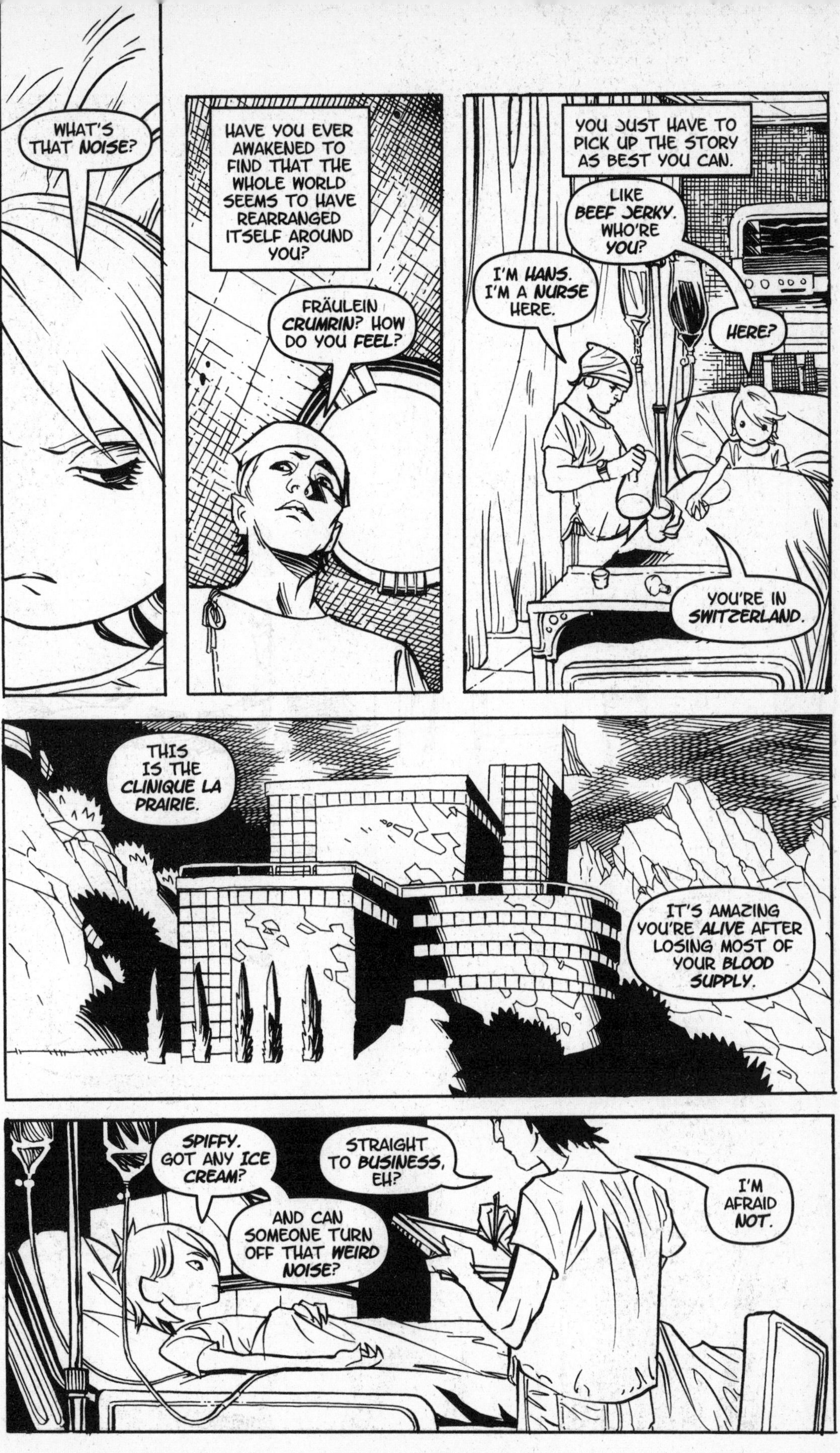

WHAT'S THAT NOISE?
HAVE YOU EVER AWAKENED TO FIND THAT THE WHOLE WORLD SEEMS TO HAVE REARRANGED ITSELF AROUND YOU?
FRÄULEIN CRUMRIN? HOW DO YOU FEEL?
YOU JUST HAVE TO PICK UP THE STORY AS BEST YOU CAN.
LIKE BEEF JERKY. WHO'RE YOU?
I'M HANS. I'M A NURSE HERE.
HERE?
YOU'RE IN SWITZERLAND.
THIS IS THE CLINIQUE LA PRAIRIE.
IT'S AMAZING YOU'RE ALIVE AFTER LOSING MOST OF YOUR BLOOD SUPPLY.
SPIFFY. GOT ANY ICE CREAM?
AND CAN SOMEONE TURN OFF THAT WEIRD NOISE?
STRAIGHT TO BUSINESS, EH?
I'M AFRAID NOT.

YOUR UNCLE *INSISTED* YOU STAY WHERE HE COULD KEEP AN EYE ON YOU.

UNFORTUNATELY, HE *SNORES* LIKE A STEAM ENGINE.

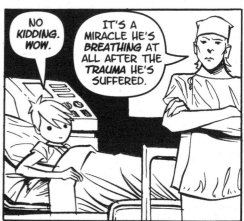

NO KIDDING. WOW.

IT'S A MIRACLE HE'S *BREATHING* AT ALL AFTER THE *TRAUMA* HE'S SUFFERED.

AND AT *HIS AGE,* TOO. MUST BE TOUGH AS *NAILS.*

HE *ALWAYS* SEEMS TO HAVE AN EXTRA *"GET OUT OF JAIL FREE"* CARD HANDY.